COLOUR JETS

Aunt Jinksie's Miracle Seeds

Shoo Rayner

Collins

COLOUR JETS

Colour Me Crazy; The Footprints Mystery; Cosmic Kev	Andrew Donkin
Captain Skywriter and Kid Wonder	Stephen Elboz
Dad on the Run	Sarah Garland
Gertie and the Bloop	Julia Jarman
Stinker Muggles and the Dazzle Bug	Elizabeth Laird
Under the Red Elephant	Jan Mark
Francis Fry, Private Eye; Francis Fry and the O.T.G.; Fishy Business for Francis Fry	Sam McBratney
Sick as a Parrot	Michaela Morgan
Harry Fly	Tasha Pym
Boys are Us	Shoo Raynor
Even Stevens F.C.	Michael Rosen
Dear Alien	Angie Sage
Reggie the Stuntman	Kate Shannon

First published in Great Britain
by HarperCollins*Publishers* Ltd 1996

The HarperCollins website address is
www.**fireandwater**.com

12 11 10 9 8 7 6 5 4 3

A CIP record for this title is available
from the British Library.

ISBN 0 00 675259 4

Printed in Hong Kong

Chapter 1

I remember the day I came home and said, "My friends think we're a strange family."

I don't think we're strange. I think my friends are just ordinary.

Us, strange? Not this family!
The term 'strange' depends on one's original reference point.
The answer is blowing in the wind.
Mum!

Mum does have her dippy moments. She's always plugged into her walkman.

Whatever she says, you can bet the words are from an old pop song.* In fact, Mum called me Juniper because of a song that she liked.

The words I have to say may be simple but they're true.

Dad seems normal, except for his cars.

We don't have a garden, it's more of a yard ... a *scrap*-yard!

Dad keeps buying old wrecks. He swears that he'll get them all going one day.

*Ask your mum (or gran) if she knows the songs.

Then there's Dad's sister, Aunt Jinksie. She's some sort of scientist and incredibly clever.

Glasses need cleaning
$(x^n \times y^n \neq z^n)$
Hair in eyes
Radiation badge
Yesterday's lunch that she's forgotten to eat
Work escaping from pocket!
Acid burns on coat
Different socks
Untied shoes

But Aunt Jinksie's not very good at real life. Because her brain is full of chemistry and maths, she finds simple things really hard. She can't even make a cup of tea without burning it!

telescope
observatory
laboratory

We thought we
might be safer from
Aunt Jinksie's experiments
if she lived in her own part of
the house.

As Dad wanted to keep the garden
free for his cars, he built her a
sort of add-on, live-in
laboratory / observatory
extension on top
of the house.

From Aunt Jinksie's observatory, you can see right across the moor to Pangloss Chemicals, where she works. Dad works there too, keeping all the machinery in order.

KEEP OUT

Pangloss Chemicals is a research station and it's a weird place. Birds don't sing there, and anything that goes near is likely to disappear, never to be seen again.

Chapter 2

One day I got flu.
I felt terrible.
My head was all thick.

My nose was all
bunged up.

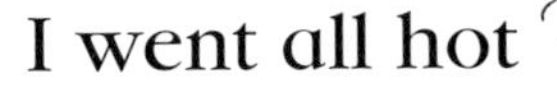

I went all hot

and cold.

I had the shakes
and shivers.

And I was so bored!

Aunt Jinksie came in to see how I was. She was in one of her helpful moods.

Hi, Nipper. I hear you're not feeling very well. Is there anything I can get you?
I wish she wouldn't call me Nipper! Juniper is bad enough.
There's a free Power Hero visor this week. All my friends will have them.
No problem. I'll add it to my shopping list. Your mum asked me to get a few things on my way to work.

I asked her to get me my *Power Hero* magazine.

Jinksie has never been much good at shopping. I slipped into a restless sleep and had nightmares about what she might buy.

This'll make a nice meal.
It's the Monster Mash!

Later, Dad brought me some tea on a tray.

You're home early.
There was an emergency at work, didn't you hear the sirens? They told us to hit the gas and head home. Jinksie might know what happened. I think it was in her department.

Outside it was now quite dark. There was a strange orange glow in the sky above the research station.

When Aunt Jinksie finally came home, she was in a very funny mood and wouldn't say what had happened at work.

Oh! It was nothing to worry about... it's all sorted out now.
I believe in miracles!
If green dot turns red shout "HELP!"

I wish someone had noticed that her radiation badge had changed colour.

Here you are, Nipper. I got your comic before I went to work. It was the last one, too.
But this is a gardening magazine.
No, it's what you asked me for. Look, I've got it written down. Magazine—Power Hero—Free Gift.
Eurgh! What's all this green, slimy stuff, Auntie?
Slimy stuff...?

I suppose I could see how she'd made a mistake. The magazine was called *Flower Power.*

HERO
R POWER
FREE GIFT
THE NEW BIG SWEET PEA FAST-GROWING!
Champion Cucumber

The word 'flower' had been covered up by the free gift – a packet of sweet pea seeds. It was a variety called Hero that was guaranteed to produce big flowers.

So, Jinksie had read:

Hero – Power – Free Gift.

That was good enough for her!

Aunt Jinksie found it hard to admit she was wrong. She huffed a bit and tried to change the subject.

What you need is fresh air. It's well known that you need fresh air for a cold.
But Jinksie, I've got flu.

She opened the window.
Freezing air rushed in.
Jinksie rushed out.

I thought I might as well look at my free gift. I emptied the seeds on to the palm of my hand and examined them.

They were all sorts of funny shapes and sizes. One of them looked like a little wasp!

ah... ah... ah...

Then something started tickling in my nose. I tried to hold it in.

It was just so... so...

I sneezed those seeds
right out of the window.
CHOOOOOOOOOO!
Mum heard and came
to see if I was all right.
Goodness! close the window. You'll catch your death of cold. Now, just knock three times on the ceiling if you want me.
Doesn't she mean the floor?

Chapter 3

I was still groggy with flu when I woke up the next day. I thought I must still be dreaming – there were birds singing outside my window.

Oooowee
chirpy
chirpy
cheep cheep.

I pulled back the curtain.
I *had* to be dreaming. There were flowers all round the window and a tropical rain forest in the yard !

Whoa! Hold on to reality, Juniper.

I realised at once that somehow my free seeds had bloomed overnight. The packet said they were fast-growing but this was ridiculous!

I woke Mum and Dad and we went outside. Aunt Jinksie was already there.

Fascinating. Incredible. Those seeds must have mutated somehow.
This can't be happening.

My cars!
Strawberry fields for ever!

It was amazing. There were some fascinating plants. Aunt Jinksie made notes about them.

There were:

twisty ones

bent ones

knobbly ones

BIG ONES

Some had bright flowers.

Some had dull flowers.

There were:

tough ones

soft ones

round ones

triangular ones

Then I found something really strange. It was wasp-coloured and had markings on the top that looked like eyes. They followed you everywhere.

Hey! I bet I know which seed this one came from.

As I bent down to get a closer look, a tendril shot out from the base of the plant and stung me on the hand.

OUCH!

OW!
Did you see that?
It stung me.

It hurt, but only
for a second.
Suddenly I felt
lighter.
I felt better. My flu had gone.

I was
CURED!

You can't exactly hide a tropical rain forest. After school my friends came to see it. I told them what had happened but I don't think they believed me.

She'll be climbing up bean stalks next.
Yeah, and talking to giants.
Hey – neat visor!
Hey – neat rain forest!

Eventually we came to the little wasp-like plant. It had grown.

Careful with this one. It stung me this morning.

As I spoke, a long, thin tendril shot out and stung Nobby Holder on the hand.
It was his warty hand.

Ouch!
Oh!

As we watched, the warts shrivelled up and disappeared.

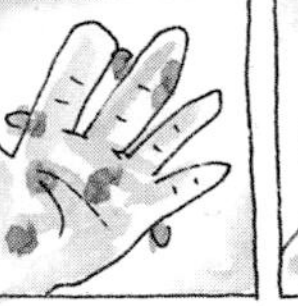

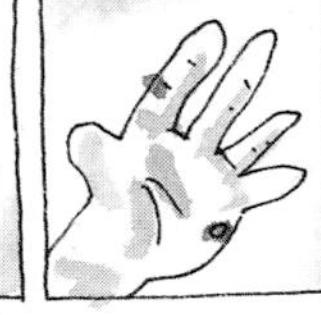

I'm not nobby any more!
Everything's gone blurred....
...Oh, that's better.

Suddenly, tendrils whipped round and stung everybody.

Then all sorts of things happened.

Noses stopped dripping,
fingernails grew,
feet stopped smelling,
and my friend Tasha found that she didn't need glasses any more.

The plant was an absolute miracle! Andy Crumley invented a name for it.

It looks like a wasp and it cures you of things. You should call it a Waspital!
Ha Ha Ha!

We told Mum about the Waspital.

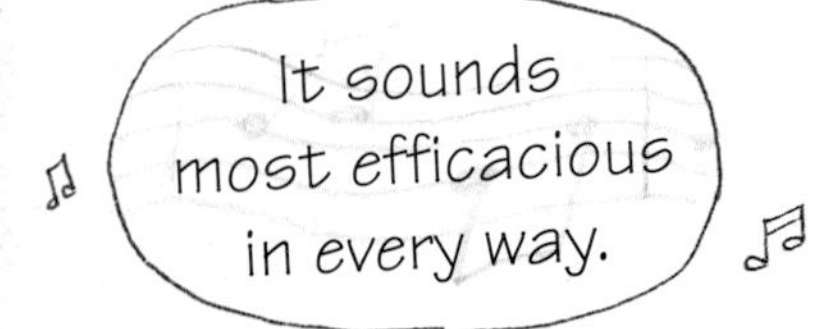
It sounds most efficacious in every way.
I wonder if she'd talk more sense if she had a little sting!

Chapter 4

It's amazing how quickly you get used to things. Within a few days I'd quite forgotten what our garden looked like before.

If you're goin' to San Francisco, Be sure to wear some flowers in your hair...
Bye Mum. See you after school.

Aunt Jinksie was very interested in the Waspital. She started making notes and taking measurements.

She asked people round to see the rain forest and got them talking about their illnesses. Then she led them to the Waspital.

It seemed to know who to sting.

And just how long have you had a bad back?
Oh, over forty years.
What's Auntie up to?

It sorted out spots, corns, bunions, water on the knee, toothache, headaches, lumbago, and things too embarrassing to talk about in public!

Andy Crumley's dad's head was as smooth as an egg until he got stung.

Overnight, a shock of thick, lustrous hair sprouted. He came round the next day and gave Aunt Jinksie a big kiss!

The Waspital even 'cured' Dad's cars! Dad was thrilled. He and Mum drove around all day, with the roof down and the radio up.

Got my motor running,
Head out on the highway....
Think I'm going back to Massachusetts.
Shocking!
J1NX

The Waspital grew and grew. One day some of the tendrils took root in the soil. Soon there were lots of tiny Waspitals.

They grew so strong that the other plants began to suffer.

Their leaves turned yellow...
...the flowers got smaller...
...and their buds dropped off.

Jinksie's next experiment was to take a little potted Waspital to the hospital.

It didn't help everyone. It couldn't mend broken bones or cure the really bad diseases, but it took the pain away and that made people feel better.

I feel great!
Me too.

Never felt better.
MORE!

Soon the newspapers, the radio and the TV heard about it. Loads of journalists came to interview Aunt Jinksie.
She was more than happy to give them her views. She became a bit of a star!

Oh it's quite simple, really. This plant obviously thrives on sickness. When it stings it actually sucks the badness out of its victim.

It's one of the most wonderful discoveries ever made. And it's a totally new species. I have named it *Waspitalis Jinksiæ*.
You're so vain.
Jinksiae? It's gone to her head.
Dad, do you think Aunt Jinksie really is a genius?
Well, she is very clever, but she never puts the lid on the toothpaste.
That's deep!

The Waspitals carried on growing, in size and in number. Soon they were taking over the town.

They got in the way sometimes, but as everyone's bad tempers were cured, no one minded.

UURRR!
Excuse me.
FRESCO

More and more of the other plants died. We should probably have been worried, but most of us were too happy.

Where have all the flowers gone?

Anyway, who needs flower displays?
We won the Best-Kept Town Competition.

Chapter 5

The day came when everyone was happy and cured of their minor ailments. Of course, that meant the Waspitals had nothing left to feed on.

They got hungry! They got cross.

One day, out of the blue, a Waspital plant stung someone for no reason.

And guess what?

It *really* hurt!

Before long you couldn't go outside without the Waspitals trying to sting you.

The happy people weren't happy any more. They got cross and tried to chop down the Waspitals.

I've been stung once too often. It's time to start pruning.
That won't help.
Every time a tendril was cut off...
it rooted to the ground...
and another Waspital grew.

You had to be careful of the sap.
It really burnt if it touched your skin.

Aunt Jinksie tried all sorts of weed killers on the Waspitals but none of them had any effect.

This really is a most unusual plant.
It's like an Octopus's garden...

The Waspitals began to get angry!
Our house was almost covered in them by now. You had to run through a tunnel of quivering, stinging tendrils to get to the front door.

Finally, the whole street was evacuated. We put what we needed into the car and went.

We've got to get out of this place,
If it's the last thing we ever do...

Everyone moved into the Sports' Centre until things could be sorted out.
We made a home for ourselves in a corner of the main hall.

Wherever I lay my hat,
That's my home...

Actually it was quite fun for a few days.
All my friends were there.

We could use the swimming pool whenever we liked, there was a coffee bar, all the other sports facilities and a disco every night.

PH

Do the hippy - hippy shake
Twist and shout!

But every day brought the Waspitals a little bit closer. People began to ask questions.

Where did these things come from?

Chapter 6

We tried to remember how it all started.

There was the accident at Pangloss Chemicals.

There was the mix-up with my magazine.

There was that green slime on Aunt Jinksie's coat, that got on to the free gift.

It can't have all been a coincidence. I wonder if the green stuff did something to the seeds?
Of course! I must get to my laboratory.

Dad and I prepared for a get-away. We got knives from the restaurant, an axe from the fire cupboard and Power Hero visors from my friends.

Come on, let's go!
I lost my heart to a starship trooper...
PH
PH
PH

Dad drove at
top speed.

SCREECH

He spun the car to a halt outside our house. We jumped out and hacked our way to the front door.

This gave us some samples of the Waspital to look at more closely.

I never promised you a rose garden.

Chapter 7

Up in her laboratory, Aunt Jinksie cut the samples into thin slices and looked at them under the microscope.

Here, hold this.
What is it?

She stuck probes into the samples and fed all sorts of data into her computer.

Suddenly I had a thought...

Aunt Jinksie – when I opened that seed packet there was a something in it that looked like a wasp. Do you think that had anything to do with it?

Jinksie thought carefully, then she got very excited.

She kept muttering "Amazing!" as she busied herself with more experiments and calculations on the computer.

Amazing! It *is* a wasp after all!
Waspitalis Jinksiæ is a cross between a wasp and a plant. Its sap is actually made of wasp stings! However, wasp-killer doesn't seem to affect it in any way.
But we've *got* to find a way to control it.

We were getting hungry. All we could find to eat were some dry biscuits and tomato ketchup.

As we were eating, Mum surprised us all by saying something that hadn't come from a song.

Bicarbonate for Bees and Vinegar for Vasps. That's how you remember it. Vinegar for wasps.
Vinegar is an antidote for wasp stings!

"Of course!" cried Jinksie.

I rushed to the larder and found the vinegar bottle. It was empty.

Oh no, what are we going to do?

Mum picked up the ketchup bottle and marched up to Aunt Jinksie's laboratory.

There's loads of vinegar in here.
58

She squirted a blob of ketchup on to a plant sample. The sample wriggled, and jiggled and finally shrivelled.

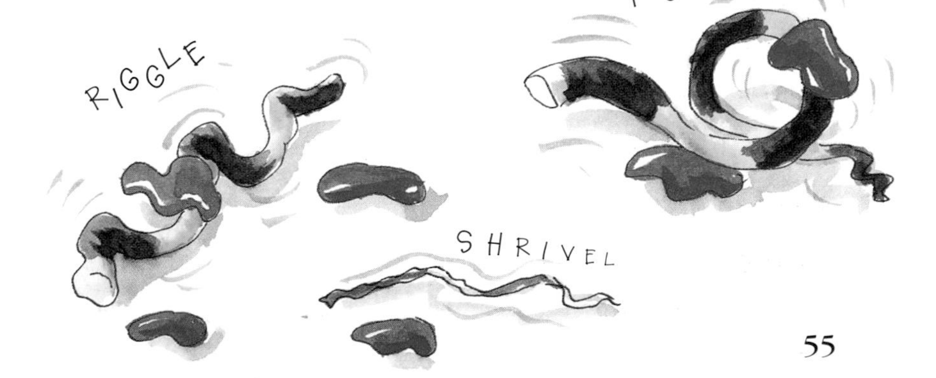
TIGGLE
RIGGLE
SHRIVEL

We hugged and danced and shouted.

It works! It works!
Let's go and tell the rest of the town.

Mum opened the front door and squirted ketchup at the menacing tendrils. The plants shrank back leaving our way clear. You could almost hear them scream!

ARGH
Lady in red...
YERG
UGH
BRRRP!

Chapter 8

We went straight to the police station and told them what we had discovered.

They found ten tomato-shaped bottles in the police canteen. Then they changed into riot gear and leapt into action.

Come on lads.
Take aim.
Fire!
BLOP!

BLURT!
FLURP!
UGH
EEK

It worked, but not well enough. When a Waspital was splattered, its tendrils dropped off and new plants instantly grew. A bigger approach was needed.

The Chief of Police made an announcement.

Make sure that you are under cover at daybreak.
Toms away!

The thin light of dawn broke, and we were woken by the drone of planes.

I looked out of the window and saw tomato ketchup falling from the sky!

SLIP!
SLOP!
SLAP!

It went on all day until the town was completely covered in ketchup and every single Waspital was destroyed.

Chapter 9

phoor!

It stank for a while, but the mushy mess soon rotted away into lovely compost and flowers grew back again.

Mum really got into horticulture and our garden is lovely now.

There is a rose in Spanish Harlem.